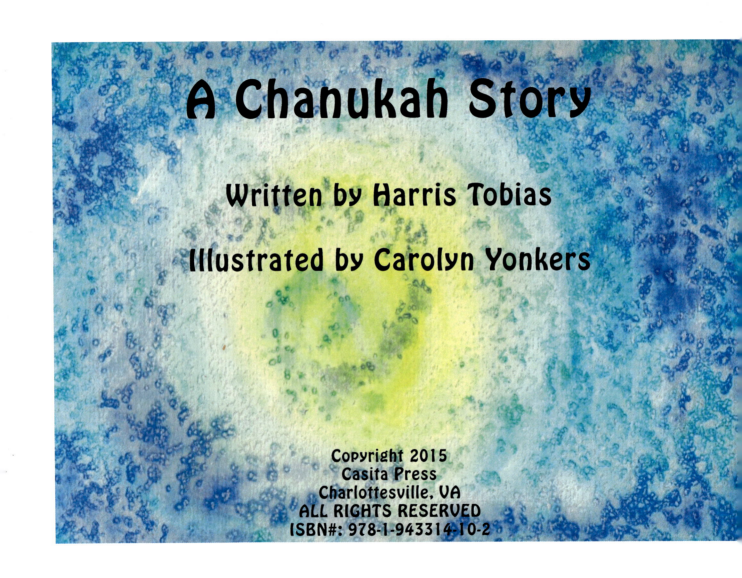

A Chanukah Story

Written by Harris Tobias

Illustrated by Carolyn Yonkers

Copyright 2015
Casita Press
Charlottesville, VA
ALL RIGHTS RESERVED
ISBN#: 978-1-943314-10-2

It was the coldest Chanukah anyone could remember. Icicles hung

from the eaves and a cold wind blew the snow into drifts on the lawn.

It was the last night of Chanukah and the fully lit menorah would do what it could to compete with the multi-colored twinkling displays of Christmas light on all the other houses in Stoney Glen Estates.

Sarah Greenstein took special pride showing the menorah in the living-room window. The menorah was a heavy silver antique passed down from her Great Grandmother.

Unfortunately, the Greenstein's menorah required a rather large, odd sized candle which had to be special ordered many weeks in advance from a Judiac store in Brooklyn.

The candles were kept in the drawer with the tablecloths until they were needed.

This is how Chanukah had been for all of Sarah's nine years. But this year something had gone wrong with the candle order. The count was wrong and the box from Brooklyn was short the nine candles needed for the last night.

stead of containing 44 candles, which covered all the nights of Chanukah, e candle box was completely empty after the seventh night. Not only were ere no special candles left, there were no candles in the house at all, and e storm outside made driving anywhere impossible.

The mood inside the Greenstein's house was as dark as the menorah.

The children played dreidel, but there was no joy in it.

All around them the neighbors' houses twinkled and flashed with Christmas color. Some houses had illuminated Santas and sleighs on their roof or lawn some had reindeer and wise men, and one had a huge inflated snowman.

Everywhere there were lights, cascades of lights hung off the roofs and engulfed every shrub and tree.

The menorah's slow build up to its fully lit splendor was all but lost in the Christmas glare.

Alas, it appeared that there was nothing to be done to salvage the situation. The festival of lights was headed for a cold and dark conclusion.

Sarah sat in her room disappointed and stared out her window.

The neighbors' colored light show reflected off the icicles hanging from the eaves giving them the appearance of colored rods.

Maybe it was that colored glow that gave Sarah the idea that saved this story and saved Chanukah for her family.

Whatever it was, Sarah was excited and needed to tell someone quickly.

Sarah ran down the steps as fast as her legs would carry her.

She ran to her father and told him her idea.

"Put icicles in the menorah?" her incredulous father asked. "I don't think that's a very good idea. They'll only melt and make a mess."

But Sarah begged and pleaded until her father put on his winter coat and went to fetch the ladder from the garage.

In a few minutes he returned with a pail containing nine icicles just about the size of the menorah's candles. Sarah set them in their sockets ready for lighting.

It looked a little strange but there was no denying that a menorah filled with icicles had a certain charm about it.

The family gathered around the curious candelabra, joined hands and said the Chanukah prayer.

Father even went as far as to light a match and touch it to the shamus, the center candle that lights the others.

No one was more surprised than the Greensteins when the icy shamus held the flame just like a real candle. In a few moments all the ice candles were li

and the menorah burned in full glory. Not only did the menorah burn all night long but, if that weren't miracle enough,

the storm knocked out all the power in Stoney Glen Estates, plunging it into darkness.

The Greenstein menorah was the only light anyone could see for miles around.

Some other books by Harris Tobias you might enjoy:
How The Cat Got Its Whiskers
The Adventures of MoonRivet
The Turtles Ball
At The Robot Zoo
Five Little Froggies
The Adventures of Rocket Bob
The King's Dream
A Wish Too Far
The Broody Little Hen
The Big Fat Counting Book
The Three Chocolatiers
The Three Swords
The Wisdom of Yaqui the Bear
The Catch of the Day
A Child's Book of Riddles
A Prisoner of Beauty
The Stone Apples
Square Sally in Circletown
A Wish Too Far
How Birds Got Their Colors
The Amulet of Power

Baker's Dozen
Bug Alphabet
Catch of the Day
Farm Song
Stinky Feet
How The Pelican Got Its Beak
How The Zebra Got Its Stripes
A Child's Book of Riddles
Snails, Scales & Animal Tales
Storyland Jack
The Three Brothers
Trumpet The Homeless Troll
And for adults and older readers:
A Felony of Birds
The Greer Agency
Alien Fruit
Chronon, Time Travel Stories
Hold The Anchovies
Peaceful Intent
The Stang
Dick Danks, The Collected Stories
Assisted